The Cottonwood Tree

BY

SERENA MANGUS

ILLUSTRATED BY

ANAIT SEMIRDZHYAN

TILBURY HOUSE PUBLISHERS, THOMASTON, MAINE

I am a teeny-tiny brown seed sleeping in a fluffy white bed.

My bed is warm and cozy as it rocks gently in the breeze, day after day.

Until one day, suddenly, I feel too hot!

POP!

Cottonwood trees live in the riparian zone that borders a lake, pond, marsh, river, or stream. This special zone creates a buffer between the aquatic ecosystem of the water body and the terrestrial ecosystem of the surrounding dry land.

Cottonwoods and other water-loving trees and shrubs sink their roots deep into the rich, moist riparian soil. They slow floodwaters, stabilize riverbanks, filter contaminated water, shade and cool the surface waters, and provide homes to birds, animals, and insects.

I join millions of other seeds, flying like snow through the air.
I float for miles and miles on the wind, drifting here and there.
Where will I stop?

Cottonwood fruit pods explode in early summer to release thousands of tiny brown seeds. Each seed is attached to soft white fibers that act like sails in the wind, helping disperse the seeds great distances from the parent tree.

Seeds that land between rocks or in crevices containing fallen leaves or soil have the best chance of growing into new trees.

At last I land on a riverbank.
I settle between the rocks and rest.
I am one of the lucky ones;
I have landed in a place where I can grow.

I am a cottonwood seed.

I stretch, cracking my seed coat.
Reaching for water, my roots grow deep into the riverbank.

I feel cramped inside my coat.
Straining with all my might, I push it off me.
I straighten my small stem, spread two little green leaves,
and stretch high into the air to bathe in the warm sun.

Every day I grow a little taller, adding more branches and
glossy green leaves. I cannot wait to be big and strong.

I am a cottonwood sprout.

Cottonwoods are among the fastest-growing trees in North America and can live 50 to 150 years or more. They can grow up to six feet a year and reach over 80 feet tall with a trunk six feet in diameter.

The largest known cottonwood
tree lived in Colorado and was
believed to be more than 300
years old. It was 105 feet tall and
36 feet around at its base!

Like other plants, cottonwood trees
create food by combining energy from
the sun with water, nutrients from the
soil, and carbon dioxide from the air.

On my first birthday, a woman and her baby visit me.
They sit beside my small branches, eating a picnic,
and watch a mother duck and her ducklings floating along the river.

The baby giggles and hugs my thin trunk.

I am a cottonwood seedling.

Mallards are among the most
common ducks throughout the world.
Female mallards usually hatch eight to
thirteen ducklings each spring. The fluffy
yellow ducklings can swim as
soon as they hatch.

On my second birthday, deer visit me.
They scratch their thick fur on my trunk, nibble my new growth,
and rest in the shade of my leaves.
I'm glad the deer don't eat all of me, and I'm glad they don't push me over!

I am a cottonwood sapling.

Deer have a big appetite for saplings. They eat leaves and young twigs. In large numbers, deer can kill a sapling by eating all the new growth or by breaking the sapling's trunk.

By my sixth birthday, I am as tall as a school bus standing on its nose! Each spring my sticky leaf buds open to reveal bright green leaves.

Young cottonwoods have thin, smooth, gray-green bark that becomes thick, rough, and deeply grooved as the tree grows older.

A little boy visits me.

He smiles as he listens to the wind rustling my leaves.

Climbing up to my lower branches, now strong enough to hold him,

he sits, nestled against my trunk.

Running his hands across my smooth bark,

he counts the ducks floating on the river.

He jumps down and gives me a hug.

He is my friend.

I am a cottonwood tree.

Only the narrowleaf cottonwood and its subspecies, the lanceleaf cottonwood, have long and narrow leaves.

Cottonwood leaves are generally triangular, with small teeth on their margins. Some take the shape of a heart.

Perching songbirds have four toes—
three pointed forward and one backward—
to help them hang onto branches.

I have other friends too.
Perching birds return each spring.
Some, like robins and warblers, tuck small,
cup-like nests among my branches. Others, like the
oriole, weave plant fibers and spider webs into
sock-like nests hanging from my limbs.

Most perching birds lay colored eggs. The young hatch featherless and blind, but they grow quickly and leave the nest within 10 to 30 days, depending on the species. Even then, the fledglings stay near their parents until they are fully independent.

Before long, these nests are filled with baby birds!
They peep, cheep, and chirp, begging their parents for food.
Soon they are fluttering from branch to branch,
protected by my canopy of leaves.

One day, they fly away to explore their own new worlds.

I am nature's nursery.
I am a cottonwood tree.

Female cottonwood trees grow green floral spikes called "catkins." Each catkin is made of numerous flowers.

By my tenth birthday,
I grow long green flowers as well as my
new leaves each spring.
The flowers become fruit pods, dressing me in
strings of green pearls that dance in the wind.
In early summer my pods burst open,
releasing tiny brown seeds wrapped in fluffy white fibers.

My cotton.

Male cottonwoods grow purple-red catkins, and these produce pollen that is carried by the wind to pollinate the female catkins.

After pollination, the female flowers develop fruit pods, and in the early summer, these release their cotton-like fluff with tiny seeds attached.

My seeds sail on the breeze up and down the river, and some will find a perfect place to settle and grow.

I am a mother now.
I am a cottonwood tree.

Some perching birds are cavity nesters, and so are many ducks and owls.

Sometimes when a strong wind howls,
a few of my branches snap and break,
leaving holes where they used to grow.
Birds, mammals, and bees arrive to nest in these holes.
Living within my hollow spaces,
my new friends take shelter and raise their young.

I am a natural condominium.
I am a cottonwood tree.

Cavity nesters are animals and birds that nest inside the trunks of trees, in holes made by birds such as woodpeckers or left by fallen branches. Common cavity nesting animals include squirrels, raccoons, opossums, and even bats.

Wild honeybees can survive many years in one tree cavity.

A teenager visits me.
As he hugs my trunk, I notice he can no longer reach all the way around me.

Climbing up into my branches, he sits in his favorite place
and runs his hands over my now bumpy bark.
I feel him relax as the wind rustles my leaves
and ducks dabble for food along the riverbank.

Grrrribbit! A loud bullfrog calls from the pond behind me.
The teenager climbs down to investigate
and gives me a pat goodbye.
He is my friend.

I am a lookout tower.
I am a cottonwood tree.

Bottoms up! Dabbling ducks feed along the surface of shallow water or by tipping headfirst into the water, leaving their tails in the air. They eat aquatic plants, vegetation, insects, and larvae.

Areas of still water occur where river water has collected and cannot easily drain. These ponds make perfect habitat for amphibians (bullfrogs and chorus frogs), reptiles (painted turtles), insects (dragonflies), and crustaceans (crawdads).

Insects climb up and down my grooved trunk
and back and forth along my branches.
Some climb into the crevices of my thick bark,
looking for a place to spin a web, a cocoon,
or hang inside a chrysalis.
Beetles drill into me, laying eggs under my bark.

Many insects live on cottonwood trees. Ants, spiders, mites, aphids, butterfly caterpillars, and others enjoy the sweet, sugary sap that runs under the bark, through the branches, and out to the tips of the leaves.

Thank goodness for the insect-eating birds that come to feast.
Thank goodness for the woodpeckers,
who peck my bark searching for beetles!

We all live in harmony, the insects, the birds, and me.

I am nature's bed and breakfast.
I am a cottonwood tree.

The cottonwood borer beetle, found in North America east of the Rocky Mountains, drills into the base of the tree and lays its eggs under the bark. When the larvae hatch, they eat the soft wood under the bark and in the tree's roots. After pupating in the root zone, the beetles chew their way out and fly away.

Cottonwood trees were used by Native Americans to mark their trails, as meeting places, and as hiding places when hunting bison. The wood was used for toys, tipi poles, ceremonial poles, and canoes. When food was scarce, cottonwood branches were fed to horses.

A young man visits me in autumn. He smiles when he
sees my bright yellow leaves swaying in the wind.

He climbs up into my strong branches
and settles into the familiar place that fits him just right.
The wind rustles my leaves while ducks preen their feathers on the riverbank.

Reading his college book out loud, he tells me how cottonwood trees were
used by Native Americans, early explorers, and pioneers
as landmarks and as a source of wood, food, and medicine.

I am glad my forebears could be of help.

The young man jumps down and gives me a pat goodbye.
He is my friend.

I am a historical icon.
I am a cottonwood tree.

*The sap of cottonwood trees contains
the same substances as modern aspirin.
Native Americans and early settlers
chewed on the bark, made a tea from the
leaves, or made a healing ointment from
the oily leaf buds in the spring.*

Beavers make dams in rivers and streams to slow the water flow, and then make lodges in the ponds the dams create. A lodge usually has two underwater entrances that lead to two dry rooms—an entrance room and a bedroom. In the wintertime, the lodge's moist walls freeze, adding insulation to keep the beaver family warm and dry.

Big beavers crisscross my roots at night.
They are always busy, gnawing on my trunk's tough outer bark,
chewing off my lower branches, or collecting those that have fallen.

Carrying my limbs to their river lodge,

they eat the nutritious wood and feed my soft twigs and leaves to their young kits.

Stacking and piling the leftover sticks,

they expand their river dam or reinforce their watertight lodge.

I am glad that I can help.

I am nature's lumberyard.

I am a cottonwood tree.

Beaver dams benefit the ecosystem by creating wetland habitat for other species, reducing flooding, filtering pollutants, and providing a nursery area for fish and warm, well-oxygenated water for frogs.

Beavers are mostly nocturnal, but you can find evidence of where they have been by looking for chew marks on trees, downed saplings, or piles of fallen branches.

A man and a young girl visit me.
The girl smiles as the wind
rustles my leaves and a pair of
ducks float on the river.

The man tells her
how I have grown in the
thirty years he has visited me.
Picking up a fallen twig, she cries,
"Look, Daddy! A star lives in the twig!"
"Yes, let me tell you the Native American tale about the stars in the cottonwood
tree." When the father is finished, the girl looks up at me with big round eyes,
"Let's come back one night when it's windy!" she exclaims.

As they leave, the father gives me a pat goodbye. He is my friend.

I am a natural legend.
I am a cottonwood tree.

"The Plains Indians, the Cheyenne and Arapaho, believe that all things come from Mother Earth. Stars are no exception. They form secretly in the earth and then drift along under the surface until they find the roots of the magical cottonwood tree.

"They enter the roots and slowly work their way up through the tree. Finally, they come to rest in the small twigs at the ends of the branches, where they wait patiently until they are needed.

"Then, when the 'Spirit-of-the-night-sky' decides she needs more beautiful stars to light up the heavens, she calls on the 'Wind-spirit' to help her. He sends wind gusts so hard that the twigs of the cottonwood tree begin to break off.

"As each twig breaks off, the stars are released and race up to a special place in the sky, where they twinkle brightly to say 'thank you.'"

I am an old tree now.

In fifty years, my boughs have become thick and strong.

Hawks build large nests in my highest branches.

A pair of bald eagles returns each year to add to their

enormous platform nest, now as heavy as a horse!

In the wintertime, their empty nests are all that can be seen in my bare branches.

I look forward to another spring,

when these magnificent birds will return to raise more chicks.

I am an aerie.

I am a cottonwood tree.

Birds of prey build huge, flat "platform nests," also known as aeries. These birds, when possible, reuse the same nest year after year, adding to its size and weight. Bald eagles build the largest nests, some weighing up to a thousand pounds!

CRASH!

Seasons come and go.
Many more years pass.
My trunk continues to grow, until
I am as wide as a pickup truck!

Kaboom!

My shape changes as the wind twists me and breaks off more and more of my old, fragile limbs. One day, the wind is too strong. It breaks me in two and sends me crashing to the ground.

Ducks come to take shelter within my fallen branches. Fish swim by, rest in the new shade, and nibble at the insects crowding around me. Some branches float downstream, getting caught in the beaver dam. Collecting this bonanza of leaves and twigs, the beavers keep their family fed and warm.

I'm glad I can still help my friends.

I am nature's benefactor.
I am a cottonwood tree.

An ecosystem is made up of living (biotic), non-living (abiotic), and dead things. A fallen tree branch, once living, is now dead but still provides food and shelter to many insects and animals. Non-living things, including air and water, shape the types of plants and animals that can live in an ecosystem.

On my eightieth birthday, an old man visits me.

He sheds a tear as he looks at my limbs in the river.

Then he notices several young sprouts growing from my roots.

He smiles.

He laughs.

He knows I am not done yet!

He is my friend.
I look forward to the day his great-
grandchildren come to visit me!

I endure.
I am a cottonwood tree.

Cottonwood trees reproduce from seeds, but
they can also reproduce by vegetative regrowth
from stumps, roots, or branches. Such regrowth is
most successful in younger trees, but older trees
with healthy, established root systems can regrow
from their roots and stumps.

Author's Note

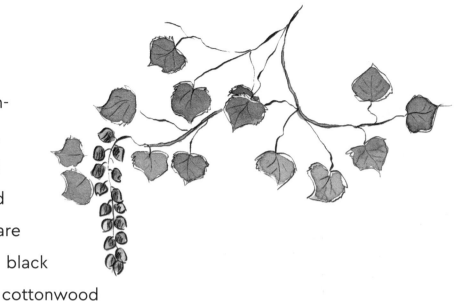

Cottonwood trees are a member of the genus *Populus*, which includes poplar and aspen trees. Five recognized species of cottonwood trees are native to the United States: black cottonwood, narrowleaf cottonwood (including its subspecies, lanceleaf cottonwood), Eastern cottonwood (including its subspecies, Plains cottonwood), Fremont cottonwood, and swamp cottonwood. I fell in love with cottonwood trees while lying under them on a riverbank one hot summer day. Almost anywhere in North America, you too can experience the joys of a cottonwood tree.

Humans have depended on cottonwood trees since North America was first inhabited thousands of years ago. Native Americans used the trees as trail landmarks and as blinds when hunting bison, while the wood was used for housing and transportation. Native Americans, early explorers, and pioneers also harvested the branches to feed livestock and to make medicinal teas and ointments. Each of these uses contributed to the success of the Corps of Discovery Expedition (1804 – 1806) led by Meriwether Lewis and William Clark, as well as the pioneers on the Oregon Trail (1811 – 1840) and Santa Fe Trail (1821 – 1880). Today, cottonwood trees make high-quality paper, pallets, crates, and boxes. Not only people benefit from cottonwood trees. Wildlife of all types depend on the trees for food and shelter.

Native American tribes use stories to explain mysteries of the universe, one of which is why cottonwood trees have star-shaped pith in their branches. Many such stories have been handed down from generation to generation with no single identified source. The story shared in these pages is one told by the Cheyenne and Arapaho people of the Great Plains.

Glossary

Abiotic: A non-living part of an ecosystem.

Aquatic: Living or growing in water.

Biotic: A living part of an ecosystem.

Ecosystem: The community of all living and non-living things in an area or habitat.

Fledgling: A young bird that has reached physical maturity but is not yet fully independent.

Habitat: The natural environment in which an organism lives.

Kit: A young beaver, fox, mink, weasel, or other fur-bearing animal.

Margin: The edges of a leaf.

Photosynthesis: The process in which plants make glucose (food) by combining the energy of the sun with water, nutrients from the soil, and carbon dioxide from the air. This process gives off oxygen.

Pupate, Pupation: The process by which an insect changes from a juvenile to an adult.

Terrestrial: Living or growing on land.

Further Reading

Cain, Kathleen. *The Cottonwood Tree*. Boulder, Colorado: Johnson Books, 2007.

Cottonwood Establishment, Survival, and Stand Characteristics. Oregon State University Extension Service, 2002.

Fact Sheets and Plant Guides. United States Department of Agriculture (USDA)/National Resources Conservation Service (NRCS).

Holling, Holling Clancy. *Tree in the Trail*. New York: Houghton Mifflin Company, 1942, renewed 1970.

Lewis and Clark Cottonwoods. North Dakota Forestry Service, Educational Handout, 2002.

Sibley, David Allen. *The Sibley Guide to Trees*. New York: Alfred A. Knopf, 2015.

Serena Mangus has a degree in Applied Ecology. As a master naturalist and certified interpretive guide in Colorado, she teaches school groups (kindergarten through high school) about flora and fauna and leads outdoor-education programs for people of all ages. She fell in love with cottonwood trees long ago on a hot day in Zion National Park—lying in their shade, watching the wind stir their leaves, hearing the splash of the river. Ever since, she seeks them out in all seasons. This is her debut book.

Anait Semirdzhyan grew up in a multicultural family and lived in several countries with diverse cultures before settling in the Seattle area with her husband and twin daughters. Her illustrations begin as pencil sketches on cold-press watercolor paper. She then inks the outlines, paints with watercolors, and scans the illustrations in order to edit them in Photoshop. She is the illustrator of *The Arabic Quilt* (Tilbury House, 2020) and other works that can be viewed at www.anaitsart.com.

Text © 2021 by Serena Mangus • Illustrations © 2021 by Anait Semirdzhyan
Hardcover ISBN 978-0-88448-856-9 • 10 9 8 7 6 5 4 3 2 1

Tilbury House Publishers • Thomaston, Maine • www.tilburyhouse.com

Library of Congress Control Number: 2021931506

Designed by Frame25 Productions
Printed in China